Rosie, the Pirate Parrot

Story by Pamela Rushby
Illustrations by Paul Könye

Contents

Chapter 1	Looking After Rosie	2
Chapter 2	Dressing Up	8
Chapter 3	The Audition	16
Chapter 4	The Lead Part	20

Chapter 1
Looking After Rosie

Ahmed pushed his baby sister's pram into their apartment building.
Grace, Jack and Lee followed closely behind him.
Mr Grimm, the caretaker of their building, thought they were babysitting.

But it wasn't a baby in the pram.
It was Rosie, a parrot with an injured wing.
The children wanted to look after the parrot until she was well again.
The problem was that their building had a rule: NO PETS. And Mr Grimm was very big on rules.

Ahmed pushed the pram towards the lift.

Looking After Rosie

The doors closed after them.
"Whew!" they said. "We're in."

"I'm going to look after Rosie first," said Jack.

The other children looked at each other.

"No, me!" said Grace.

"Me!" said Lee.

"It's my pram!" said Ahmed.

"All right," Jack said.
"The fairest way is to play 'Scissors, Paper, Rock'."
He put his hands behind his back.
"Ready, Lee?" he asked.

Grace won the game.

"But you only keep Rosie for two days," the boys said. "Then it's our turn."

"We'll have to ask our parents if it's all right to keep Rosie," Lee said.
"I'm not sure what my dad will say."

"Will your mum say it's okay, Grace?" asked Ahmed.

"I hope so," Grace replied.

Chapter 2
Dressing Up

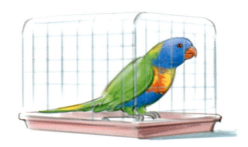

Grace's mum thought Rosie was beautiful. She bought some birdseed and Grace fed Rosie that night, and again in the morning.

"Cup of tea?" Rosie squawked. "Bill?"

"You need to get ready for school now, Grace," said Mum.
"Don't forget it's the audition for the school play today. It's about pirates, isn't it? Have you learned your lines?"

Dressing Up

Grace frowned. "I don't want to do the audition," she said.

"I don't like standing up in front of everyone. And the boys in my class say girls can't be pirates."

"Then they're wrong," Mum said.
"There were some very famous women pirates."

"Were there?" Grace said.
"Well, perhaps I should try, then."

"I think you should," Mum said.
"Would it help if you dressed up?
I could find some big earrings and a head scarf
and you could wear your boots."

Soon, Grace looked like a pirate.

"Fantastic!" said Mum. "You look really scary! Will you have a go at the audition now?"

Grace sighed. "I just don't want to do it by myself."

"Cup of tea?" squawked Rosie. "Bill?"

Grace and Mum looked at Rosie.
"All the best pirates have parrots on their shoulders," said Mum.

"Maybe I won't have to do it all by myself!" Grace said.

Grace ran to Ahmed's apartment
and borrowed the pram.
As she pushed it out the front door of the building,
Mr Grimm saw her.

"Babysitting again, are you?" he said. "That's good! I like to see children helping. It keeps them out of trouble!"

Grace smiled to herself.

Chapter 3

The Audition

Grace wanted to keep Rosie a surprise
for the boys in her class.
She asked her teacher, Ms Green,
if she could keep Rosie's cage
in the teachers' lunch room all day.
Ms Green thought that would be all right.

When it was time for the audition,
Grace pushed the pram into the school hall.
Ms Green and Mr Smitt were waiting
to hear the children audition.

"Huh!" said one of the boys in Grace's class,
"a pirate with a baby? What kind of a pirate is that?"

The Audition

Grace waited quietly for her turn.
She still felt scared about going up onto the stage and saying her lines.

"Grace!" called Ms Green. "It's your turn now!"

Rosie, the Pirate Parrot

Grace opened the cage and took Rosie out.
Rosie sat happily on Grace's shoulder.
Grace took a deep breath
and marched up onto the stage.

"Wow!" said the boys in her class.
"Look at that! She's got a real parrot!"

Grace started her lines.
"Shiver my timbers!" she shouted.
"Who dares to steal Captain Kidd's treasure?"

Rosie joined in with a little squawk
and flutter.

Chapter 4

The Lead Part

Grace was the only pirate at the audition with a real parrot on her shoulder.

"That's wonderful!" Ms Green said. "Does your parrot say things like 'Pieces of eight'?"

"No," said Grace, "only 'Cup of tea?' and 'Bill'!"

The teachers laughed.
"Well, you've got the lead part, anyway!" Mr Smitt said.

The Lead Part

Grace put Rosie back in the cage and into the pram, then she walked quickly home to tell Mum.

"That's fantastic!" Mum said. "I'm so proud of you!"

"I'm still scared about standing up
in front of all those people," Grace said.
"But at least I won't have to do it all by myself!"

The Lead Part

Rosie flapped her good wing.
"Cup of tea?" she squawked. "Bill?"